D1518732

Nature's Super Secrets

# How Do Eggs Hatch?

By Elena Hobbes

Gareth Stevens
Publishing

**Please visit our website, www.garethstevens.com. For a free color catalog of all our high-quality books, call toll free 1-800-542-2595 or fax 1-877-542-2596.**

Library of Congress Cataloging-in-Publication Data

Hobbes, Elena
How do eggs hatch? / by Elena Hobbes.
cm. – (Nature's super secrets)
Includes bibliographical references and index.
Summary: Brief text and photographs tell how baby chicks develop and hatch from eggs.
Contents: All about eggs – Hens – Inside the egg – Hatching.
ISBN 978-1-4339-8161-6 (pbk.)
ISBN 978-1-4339-8162-3 (6-pack)
ISBN 978-1-4339-8160-9 (hard bound)
1. Eggs—Juvenile literature    2. Chickens—Development—Juvenile literature
3. Chicks—Juvenile literature    [1. Eggs    2. Chickens]    I. Title
        2013
636.5—dc23

Published in 2013 by
**Gareth Stevens Publishing**
111 East 14th Street, Suite 349
New York, NY 10003

Designer: Michael J. Flynn
Editor: Sarah Machajewski

Photo credits: Cover Photodisc/Getty Images; p. 5 (speckled eggs) Asturianu/Shutterstock.com; p. 5 (chicken eggs) stocknadia/Shutterstock.com; p. 5 (robin eggs) D&D Photos/Shutterstock.com; pp. 7, 21 (chick) Steshkin Yevgeniy/Shutterstock.com; pp. 9, 21 (eggs in nest) Aprilphoto/Shutterstock.com; pp. 11, 21 (hen) Regina Chayer/Shutterstock.com; p. 13 mocagrande/Shutterstock.com; pp. 15, 21 (embryo) © iStockphoto.com/OnyxRain; p. 17 © iStockphoto.com/Yarinca; pp. 19, 21 (hatching) saied shahin kiya/Shutterstock.com; p. 21 (nest) Brooke Becker/Getty Images.

Printed in the United States of America

CPSIA compliance information: Batch #CW13GS: For further information contact Gareth Stevens, New York, New York at 1-800-542-2595.

# Table of Contents

**Boldface** words appear in the glossary.

# All About Eggs

Have you ever seen an egg? Eggs can be big or small. They can be many different colors. Some of them even have spots! Many baby animals grow inside eggs. Eggs **hatch** when the animals are born.

Chickens come from eggs. Baby chickens are called chicks. It takes three weeks for a chick to hatch from an egg. A lot happens in that time! The chick grows and grows until it's ready to be born.

# Hens

Chicken eggs are shaped like ovals. They have a thin shell and can break easily. Eggs come from **female** chickens, called hens. The hens lay their eggs in a nest made of straw.

Hens take good care of their eggs. They sit on the eggs until they hatch. This keeps the eggs safe and warm. Eggs need to stay very warm for the chicks to grow. They won't hatch if they get cold.

11

Hens also have to turn the eggs until they hatch. Hens turn the eggs with their beaks. This helps the chicks grow the right way. We can't see the chicks, but they get bigger every day.

13

# Inside the Egg

Inside the shell, the egg has a yellow **yolk** and a white **liquid**. The chicks use these as food. In a few weeks, there's no more liquid inside the egg. The chicks take up all the space!

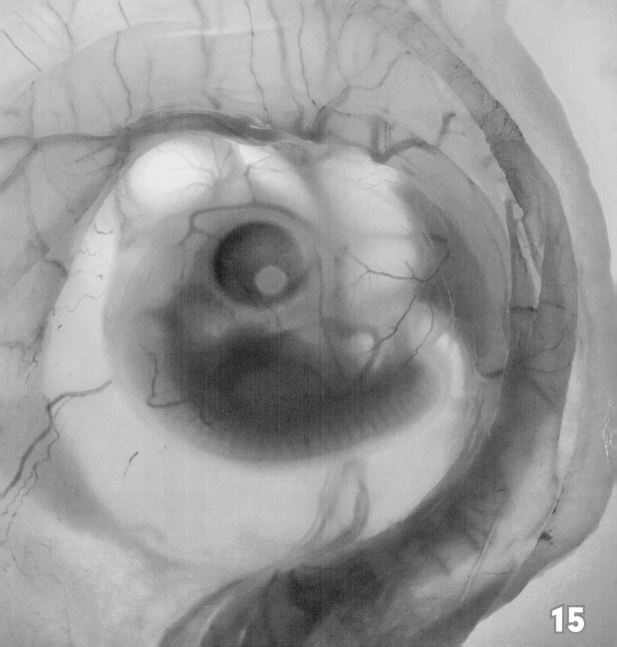

**15**

We can't see the chicks, but we can hear them! They make a soft peeping sound from inside the egg. The peeping tells their mom they're ready to hatch. You can hear it, too, if you listen closely.

17

# Hatching

Chicks use their necks to lift their heads to the shell. Their necks are very strong. Then, they break the shell with their **egg tooth**. An egg tooth is a sharp point on the end of a beak.

The chicks break the shell until they're all the way out. After they hatch, chicks need water, food, and warmth. They have soft yellow feathers. When they grow up, they become adult chickens!

The hen lays eggs.

The hen keeps the eggs warm in a nest.

Finally, the chicks hatch!

**Hatching an Egg**

The chicks break the shell with their egg tooth.

The chicks grow bigger.

21

# Glossary

**egg tooth:** a sharp point on the end of a beak that is used for hatching

**female:** a girl

**hatch:** to break open or come out of

**liquid:** something that flows and takes the shape of the container holding it

**yolk:** the yellow part of an egg that the chick uses for food

# For More Information

## Books

Kant, Tanya. *How an Egg Grows into a Chicken.* Danbury, CT: Children's Press, 2009.

Sklansky, Amy E. *Where Do Chicks Come From?* New York, NY: Harper Collins, 2005.

## Websites

**Baby Chicks Hatching**
*www.msichicago.org/online-science/videos/video-detail/activities/the-hatchery/*
Watch chicks hatch in this fascinating video from Chicago's Museum of Science and Industry!

**Egg and Embryo Development**
*www.enchantedlearning.com/subjects/birds/info/chicken/egg.shtml*
Read about how eggs form and learn key vocabulary related to egg development.

**Publisher's note to educators and parents:** Our editors have carefully reviewed these websites to ensure that they are suitable for students. Many websites change frequently, however, and we cannot guarantee that a site's future contents will continue to meet our high standards of quality and educational value. Be advised that students should be closely supervised whenever they access the Internet.

# Index